Printed in the United States of America.
For information address Disney Press,
114 Fifth Avenue, New York, New York 10011.

First Edition
1 3 5 7 9 10 8 6 4 2

Library of Congress Catalog Card Number 94-71797
ISBN 0-7868-3041-7 / 0-7868-5031-0 (lib. bdg.)